Believe It or Not, my Brother has a Monster!

By
Kenn Nesbitt

Pictures by
David Slonim

Cartwheel Books
An Imprint of Scholastic Inc.

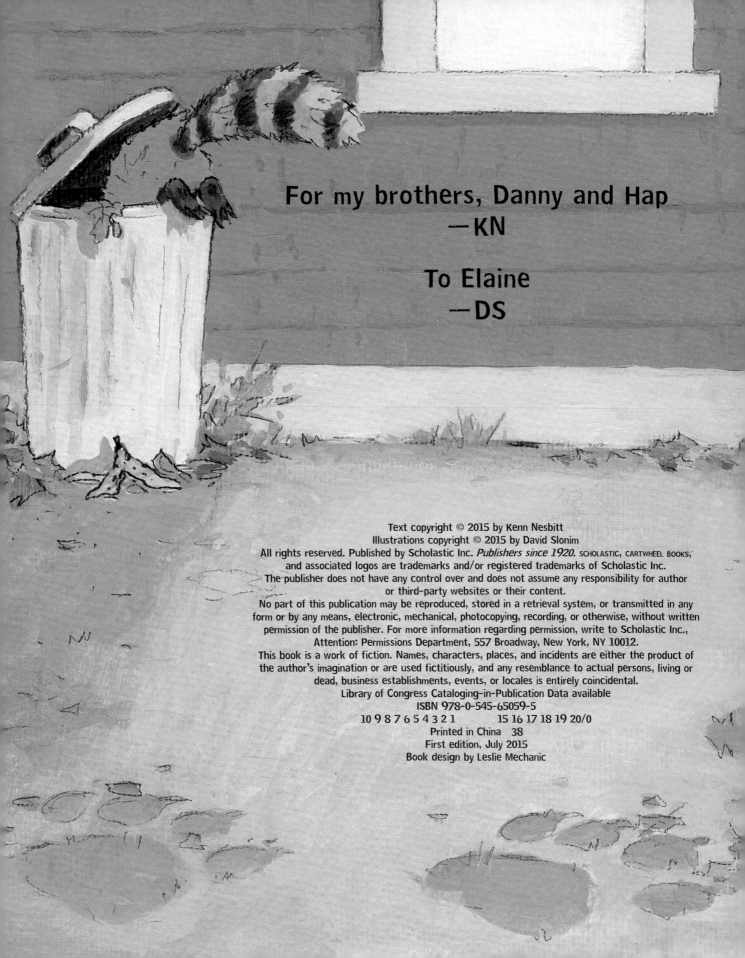

For my brothers, Danny and Hap
—KN

To Elaine
—DS

Text copyright © 2015 by Kenn Nesbitt
Illustrations copyright © 2015 by David Slonim

Library of Congress Cataloging-in-Publication Data available
ISBN 978-0-545-65059-5
10 9 8 7 6 5 4 3 2 1   15 16 17 18 19 20/0
Printed in China   38
First edition, July 2015
Book design by Leslie Mechanic

It happened just last Halloween,
the weirdest thing you've ever seen:
My brother went out after dark
and found a monster in the park.

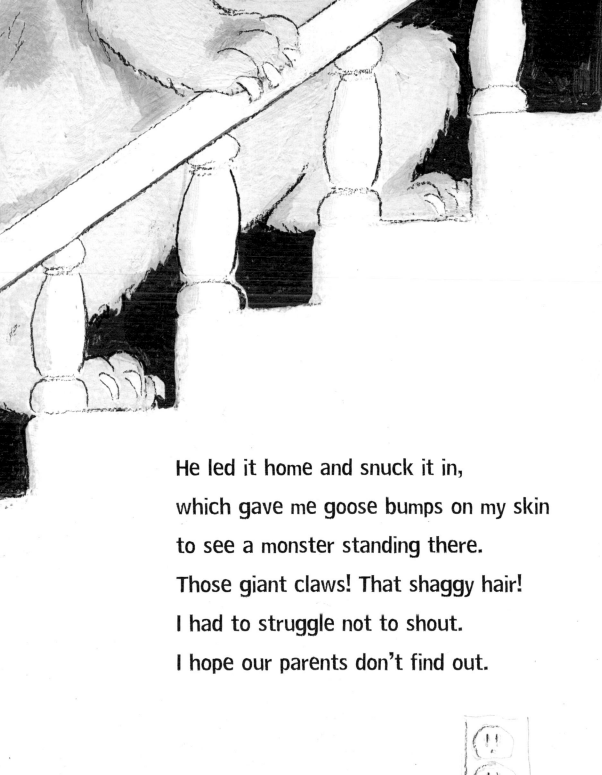

He led it home and snuck it in,

which gave me goose bumps on my skin

to see a monster standing there.

Those giant claws! That shaggy hair!

I had to struggle not to shout.

I hope our parents don't find out.

I felt a sense of dread and doom
within my brother's darkened room.
My pounding heart began to race,
and when he saw my frightened face,
my brother flew back out and found
two hairy spiders, big and round.
He set them gently on his bed.
They crawled up on the monster's head,
then crept along its scruffy snout.
I hope our parents don't find out.

Although they gave me chills and sweats,

my brother liked his creepy pets.

So when he spied three rats outside,

he brought them in. I nearly cried!

He dropped them in his dresser where

they snatched his socks and underwear.

The spiders thought the rats were fun;

who knew that underwear could run?

The monster chased them all about.

I hope our parents don't find out!

Four toads he captured bounced a ball
around the room and off the wall.
The rats jumped in to join the fun.
The spiders bounced another one.
Oh, goodness, what a crazy night!
The balls went flying left and right
and bonked the monster on the snout.
I hope our parents don't find out!

He next found five black cats that night.

I felt so scared, my face went white.

The instant that he let them go

they powered on his stereo.

The spiders did the "Monster Mash."

The toads and rats enjoyed the bash.

The monster bopped and flopped about.

I hope our parents don't find out!

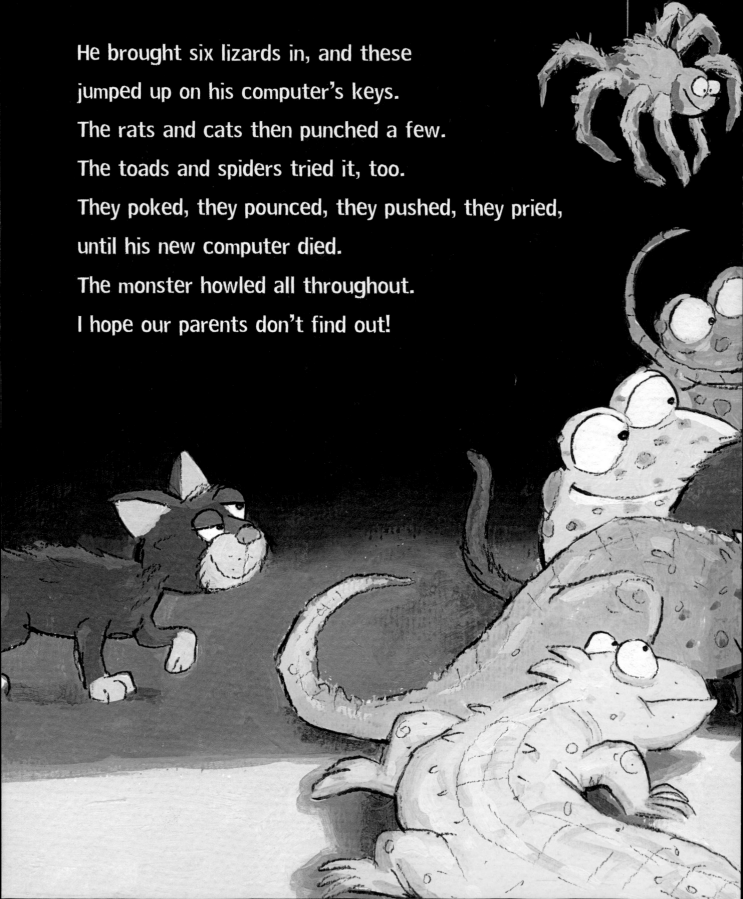

He brought six lizards in, and these
jumped up on his computer's keys.
The rats and cats then punched a few.
The toads and spiders tried it, too.
They poked, they pounced, they pushed, they pried,
until his new computer died.
The monster howled all throughout.
I hope our parents don't find out!

He then snuck seven bats inside.

The spiders ran and tried to hide.

They dashed behind some picture frames,

and dumped the box with all his games.

The lizards dove to dodge the bats,

who chased the toads and rats and cats,

and swooped around the monster's snout.

I hope our parents don't find out!

The eight black ravens that he found
flew in and raced the bats around.
The spiders, toads, and lizards, too,
climbed up to get a better view.
The rats and cats all shrieked to see
the bats crash into his TV.
The monster grinned, without a doubt.
I hope our parents don't find out!

My brother really must like bugs,

for next came nine disgusting slugs.

He put them down, and right away,

those slimy slugs began to play.

They took his skateboard for a spin,

and THAT'S when Mom and Dad walked in.

They instantly switched on the light,
and this is what they saw that night:

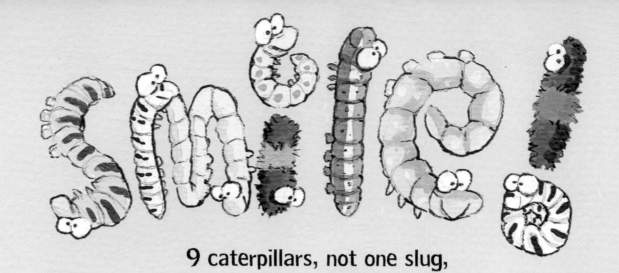

9 caterpillars, not one slug,

8 robins strutting on the rug,

plus 7 lovely butterflies,

6 geckos with big, friendly eyes,

5 kittens on the stereo,

4 frogs all croaking in a row,

3 mice inside a dresser drawer,

2 gerbils playing on the floor,

and, looking not the least bit scary,
1 shaggy dog, just big and hairy.

But when he saw our parents frown
he started jumping up and down.
He yipped and bounced and acted wild.
Our parents patted him and smiled.

The kittens then began to purr.
Our parents felt their fluffy fur.

They pet the geckos, frogs, and mice,
and said the butterflies were nice.

The robins chirped a silly song.

Our parents whistled right along.

They brushed the gerbils and, it's true,

they held the caterpillars, too.

And Mom and Dad had such a ball,

they told him he could keep them all!

You'd think he'd be completely set
and never need another pet,
and yet, today he found ten snakes.
Ten garter snakes, for goodness' sakes!
And snakes he cannot do without . . .

I hope our parents don't find out.